ORCHARD BOOKS

First published in the USA by Scholastic Inc in 2017
First published in the UK in 2017 by The Watts Publishing Group

7 9 10 8

A CIP catalogue record for this book is available from the British Library.

ISBN 978 1 40835 368 4

Printed and bound in Great Britain

The paper and board used in this book are
made from wood from responsible sources.

Orchard Books
An imprint of Hachette Children's Group
Part of The Watts Publishing Group Limited
Carmelite House, 50 Victoria Embankment, London EC4Y 0DZ

An Hachette UK Company

www.hachette.co.uk
www.hachettechildrens.co.uk

Which Pokémon will you find in this adventure?
Turn to the back when you have spotted them!

ASH'S BIG CHALLENGE

Adapted by Tracey West

ORCHARD

CHAPTER 1

A NEW JOURNEY

"Ash, I need you to run a very important errand for me," Professor Oak said.

Ash Ketchum beamed. Here he was back in Pallet Town in the lab of Professor Oak, one of the world's greatest Pokémon experts. He was surrounded by his best friends, Misty and Brock. Pikachu, his favourite Pokémon, sat on his shoulder. And now Professor Oak was entrusting him with an important mission. Ash felt proud.

"Of course, I asked my grandson Gary to go," Professor Oak said, "but he was busy."

Ash cringed. He should have guessed he was second choice after Gary. Gary had begun his Pokémon training at the same time as Ash and was his top rival.

"What's the errand?" Misty asked.

"I need you to go to Valencia Island in the Orange Archipelago," Professor Oak said.

"The Archipela-who?" Ash asked.

But Misty and Brock looked excited.

"Valencia! It's beautiful there," Misty said.

"Yeah," Brock said. "And there are lots of girls on the beach."

"My friend Professor Ivy works there," the professor continued. "She recently acquired

a mysterious Poké Ball. I'd like you to bring it to me so that I can study it."

"Can't you just have her transport it to you like any other Poké Ball, Professor?" Misty asked. Trainers from Pallet Town often transported Pokémon in their Poké Balls to Professor Oak's lab. Because Trainers can only carry six Pokémon at a time, he helped them raise any extra Pokémon they caught.

"We've tried to transport the Poké Ball, but it doesn't work," Professor Oak said. "That's one of the reasons it's so mysterious."

Ash liked the sound of that. "Of course I'll go, Professor," he said.

"Me, too," said Misty and Brock together.

Professor Oak smiled. "Wonderful!" he said. "I know I can count on all of you."

Ash and his friends started out on their journey the next morning. Brock carried a pack filled with special Pokémon food.

Brock looked tough, but he knew a lot about caring for Pokémon.

Misty held Togepi, her baby Pokémon. Pikachu walked alongside Ash. Its lightning-bolt tail bobbed up and down. They trekked through the forest in silence, but Ash's mind was crowded with thoughts.

Ash was ten years old when he first began his journey as a Pokémon Trainer in Professor Oak's lab. A lot had happened since then. He had fought Gym Leaders in eight different towns and earned badges from all of them. He had even competed in the Pokémon League, where he finished in the top sixteen. Not bad.

And most important, he was learning how to become a good Pokémon Trainer. He had caught and trained many different types of Pokémon. Some of them had even evolved into higher forms. Charmander had evolved into Charmeleon and then Charizard. Pidgey, his Flying-type Pokémon, had recently evolved into Pidgeot.

Ash was learning more each day. And now Professor Oak had entrusted him with an important mission. He couldn't wait!

Ash and his friends walked for hours. Eventually, Ash saw the crystal blue ocean twinkling in the sunlight.

"All right!" Ash said. "We'll be on Valencia Island in no time."

Brock flipped through a guidebook. He frowned.

"I've got bad news, Ash," Brock said. "According to this, we'll have to sail for weeks to get anywhere near the island!"

CHAPTER 2

TOO GOOD TO BE TRUE

"Weeks!" Ash cried.

Brock flipped through the book. "If we go by blimp, it will take less than a day," he said. "But the blimp is pretty expensive."

Ash turned out his pockets. He had a few coins but not enough for a blimp ride.

"I wish we had enough money to go by

blimp," Ash said. "Don't you, Pikachu?"

"Pika!" The yellow Electric-type Pokémon nodded in agreement.

Ash sighed. "I'd better go buy some food and supplies for our trip," he said.

Pikachu, Misty and Brock followed Ash to the store down the road. Ash bought enough snacks to fill his knapsack. When he left, he noticed two men standing behind a table in front of the store. A banner draped over the table read, "You Can Be a Winner!"

One of the men called to Ash. "Bring your register receipt here and take a chance. You could win a free blimp ride to beautiful Valencia Island!"

"Did he say 'blimp'?" Brock asked. "This sounds too good to be true."

"Who cares?" Ash said. "Let's try."

Ash handed his receipt to the men. One

of them spun a round cage with yellow balls inside. When the cage stopped moving, a single ball fell into the man's hand.

He looked at the ball, then at the receipt.

"Congratulations!" the man said. "You have won our grand prize round-trip blimp flight to Valencia Island!"

Misty and Brock couldn't believe it.

"There's something weird about this," Misty said.

"Yeah," Brock agreed. "Those two seem kind of familiar."

Ash didn't care. "We're just lucky!" he said. "Let's get going!"

The blimp yard was only a short walk away. Ash had seen blimps in the sky before. They usually gleamed bright silver.

But no beautiful silver blimp waited for them. Instead, a dirty grey blimp sat in the

yard. It looked like it was falling apart.
Ash saw two men in work uniforms in the
blimp yard. He approached them.

"Is this the blimp to Valencia Island?" Ash
asked.

One of the workers, a short man with a
moustache, raised his eyebrows. "You're not
here for a blimp ride, are you?" he asked.

"Yes, sir," Ash said. "We won tickets."

The other worker looked shocked. "How much are you getting paid?"

"Paid?" Ash asked. "What do you mean?"

The worker with the moustache looked around cautiously. "Everyone knows that blimp is haunted," he said in a loud whisper. "I wouldn't fly on that thing if you paid me a million bucks!"

Ash started to reply, but a voice from a loudspeaker filled the air.

"Attention, please," the voice blared. "Passengers may now begin boarding the blimp to Valencia Island."

Ash looked up. A man in a blue pilot's uniform and a woman in a blue flight attendant's uniform stood at the top of a stairway leading to the entrance of the blimp.

Ash climbed the stairs. "What about the ghosts?" Ash asked the pilot.

"Ghosts?" the pilot asked. "There are no ghosts on this blimp. How silly!"

"But those men down there said this blimp was haunted," Misty said from behind Ash.

The flight attendant laughed. "They must be from a rival blimp line. Get on board!"

She pushed Ash and his friends inside.

They walked down a dim hallway into a large room. The room looked like a dining room, but it was a mess. Dust covered a long table in the centre of the room. Torn red curtains drooped on the walls.

Misty shuddered. "This place sure looks like it's haunted," she said.

Ash shook his head. "Stop worrying. We'll be on Valencia Island before you know it. I can't wait to get there!"

In the next room, the pilot and flight attendant laughed. They took off their blue uniforms to reveal white costumes emblazoned with a red letter R.

They were Jessie and James from Team Rocket!

"This is too good to be true," Jessie said. "First we tricked them into taking tickets from us. Then we convinced them to climb aboard this old blimp. Now we have the perfect opportunity to steal Ash's Pikachu."

"Of course," James said. "But what were they babbling about? The Boss never said this blimp was haunted."

"This blimp isn't haunted," said Jessie. That's ridiculous."

"Meowth! Don't be so sure!"

Jessie and James turned. It was Meowth, their talking Scratch Cat Pokémon.

"What are you talking about?" James asked.

"If this ship isn't haunted," Meowth said, "then who's piloting the blimp?"

Panicked, Jessie and James looked out a nearby window.

"Oh, no!" Jessie cried. "The blimp is taking off!"

CHAPTER 3

A SCARE IN THE AIR

"Cool! We're on our way," Ash said as the blimp groaned and rose into the air.

The blimp rocked back and forth as it moved through the sky.

Misty held Togepi tightly. "We're moving, all right. I just don't really like *how* we're moving."

Ash leaned back in his seat and put his arms behind his head. "Relax, Misty," he said. "This ride's going to be – whoaaa!"

The blimp lurched forward. Ash yelled as he flew off his seat and landed on the floor with a thud. Dazed, he saw Misty and Brock sprawled on the floor next to him. Pikachu rolled across the blimp, just out of his grasp.

"What's happening?" Misty screamed.

"I'm not sure," Ash answered. "It feels like the blimp is tilted – whoaaa!"

The blimp rocked again. This time the blimp tilted backward. Ash felt himself sliding across the floor again.

Crash! They all bumped into the back wall.

The blimp creaked. "Oh, no," Ash said. "Not again!"

The blimp started to move. Ash braced

for the worst. The blimp tilted again, then straightened. They were level.

Ash rubbed his head and stood up.

"Is everyone OK?" he asked.

"I guess so," Misty replied. "How are you doing, Toge—" Misty gasped.

Ash looked. Instead of Togepi in her arms, there was a pillow!

"Togepi's disappeared!" Misty cried.

While Misty panicked in the main room, Team Rocket panicked in the control room.

"Can't you do a better job of flying this thing?" Jessie snarled.

Meowth furiously pawed through an instruction book.

"Meowth! I'm doing the best I can," the Pokémon replied.

"Well, so far all you've done is make me dizzy," James complained.

"We're all right now," Meowth said.

James pointed. "Maybe not. Look!"

A dark storm cloud loomed in front of the ship.

"We've got to do something!" Jessie cried.

Meowth pointed to a red button on the control panel. "If we press the emergency button, the gas will be let out of the blimp. We'll land in the ocean."

"We can't mess up this mission," James said. "The Boss will be so disappointed."

Jessie looked thoughtful. "It doesn't matter," she said. "As long as we capture Pikachu, the Boss won't care if we sink this stupid blimp or not."

"You're right, Jessie," James said. "We'll be heroes."

"So let's forget about steering this blimp, and let's start stealing Pikachu!" Jessie cried.

While Team Rocket raced off to find Pikachu, Ash and his friends raced around trying to find Togepi.

Their search took them inside the frame of the blimp. Metal beams and staircases surrounded them. It reminded Ash of a big skeleton.

"What would Togepi be doing in a creepy place like this?" Ash asked.

"It's the only place we haven't looked yet," Brock said.

Misty looked worried. "Togepi! Where are you?"

Ash strained to see in the dim light.

Togepi was nowhere in sight.

Then something darted across one of the metal beams.

Something small.

"Hey, did you guys see that?" Ash asked.

Misty nodded. "Maybe it was Togepi!"

Ash chased after the figure. His friends followed.

There it was again.

A small flash of white.

Ash climbed one of the ladders. He could see the figure more clearly now on one of the beams below.

"There it is!" Ash yelled.

Misty, Brock, and Pikachu crowded around Ash.

"Togepi?" Misty asked.

Thunder boomed. A flash of lightning lit up the area.

The figure wasn't Togepi. It was all white, with a flowing body, no face, and arms extended in front of it.

"A ghost!" Ash cried.

CHAPTER 4

BATTLE OF THE BLIMP

"I guess this blimp really is haunted," Brock said.

Ash watched in disbelief as the ghost floated away.

"This whole blimp must be full of ghosts," Ash said. "I think we should try to get off this thing."

"We can't get off," Brock pointed out. "We're a mile above the ground."

Misty shook her head. "I'm not leaving here without Togepi," she said. "I'll battle ghosts or anybody else if I have to!"

"That's our cue!" a voice cried.

Ash spun around.

The voice belonged to Jessie of Team Rocket. She, James and Meowth had climbed down a ladder and entered the frame of the blimp.

"Not again!" Ash groaned. Team Rocket was always setting traps to try to steal Pikachu from him. Ash couldn't believe he had fallen into another one.

Misty was angry. "We have more important things to worry about now," she told them. "So go away!"

"We're not going anywhere!" James replied.

"And you're not going anywhere, either," Jessie snarled.

Meowth glared at Ash. "Nobody's leaving this balloon until we get what we want!" Meowth threatened. "Now hand over that Pikachu!"

Jessie took a red-and-white Poké Ball from her belt.

"Arbok, go!" she cried, tossing the ball in the air.

James threw a Poké Ball, too.

"Weezing, showtime!" he yelled.

A bright flash of light filled the blimp,

 and two Pokémon appeared. Weezing, a Poison-type Pokémon, looked like a dark cloud of gas with two heads. Arbok, Jessie's

Pokémon, looked like a large purple snake.

"Arbok, use your Bite attack!" Jessie commanded.

Ash reacted quickly.

"Pikachu, Thunder Shock now!" he ordered.

Pikachu didn't hesitate. The yellow Pokémon built up an electric charge in its body, then released it into the air.

The shock tore through Arbok. But sparks also hit the metal frame of the blimp. Everyone touching the frame got shocked, too.

"Ash, you can't use shock attacks in a blimp!" Misty yelled.

"Good point," Ash admitted.

"No problem," Brock said. "Geodude, go!"

Brock threw a Poké Ball, and a Pokémon that looked like a small boulder with two small, muscular arms appeared.

Weezing flew through the air, headed

straight for Geodude. Geodude jumped up. It grabbed Weezing like a basketball and threw the Poison-type Pokémon with all its might.

Weezing crashed into the canvas wall covering the blimp, tearing a jagged hole in the material. Through the hole, Ash could see a wild storm raging outside.

It was all too much. A ghost. A Team

Rocket attack. And now a storm. Ash didn't know what to worry about first.

"Togepi!" Misty yelled.

Ash looked. He had forgotten all about Togepi. The tiny Pokémon was toddling along on one of the high steel beams that held the blimp together.

"Let's go!" Misty said. She climbed up one of the ladders to get Togepi.

Ash didn't think twice. He followed Misty up the ladder. Pikachu and Brock were right behind him.

Togepi kept walking along the steel beam next to the hole Weezing had torn in the canvas. There was nothing between Togepi and the storm raging outside.

Misty climbed up the stairs, determined to save Togepi.

"Misty, you can't go out there!" Ash said.

"I know," Misty replied. "But Bulbasaur can help me keep my balance."

"Right," Ash said. He took out Bulbasaur and released it. "Bulbasaur, I choose you!"

A Grass- and Poison-type Pokémon that looked like a small dinosaur with a plant bulb on its back appeared.

"Bulbasaur, use your attack Vine Whip to save Misty," Ash commanded.

"Bulbasaur!" the Pokémon replied. The plant bulb on its back opened up, and two long green vines shot out. The vines snaked up and wrapped around Misty.

With Bulbasaur keeping her steady, Misty tiptoed out on to the steel beam. She took one small step after another. Rain and wind lashed at her face.

Ash held his breath. Togepi was just a few feet away from him.

"Come on, Togepi," Misty pleaded.

Suddenly, something small and white jumped between Misty and Togepi. The ghost!

Before Misty could react, a strong gust of wind blew. Something white fluttered off the  ghost. Ash thought it looked like a sheet.

And underneath the sheet was ... Jigglypuff!

Ash didn't know whether or not to be relieved at the sight of Jigglypuff. The round pink Pokémon wasn't as scary as a ghost, but it was just as troublesome. Jigglypuff loved to sing, and its song put anyone who heard it right to sleep.

Jigglypuff was happy to have an audience. It hopped up and down. It took a deep breath, like it always did when it was about to sing.

"Jigglypuff, no!" Misty cried.

Ash covered his ears. What else could happen?

A loud groan answered his question. The blimp was out of control again. The huge airship tilted forward sharply.

Ash and Brock each grabbed hold of a ladder. Pikachu clung to Ash's back.

On the beam above, Misty leaned forward and quickly scooped up Togepi. Bulbasaur's strong vines kept Misty from falling off the beam.

Team Rocket wasn't so lucky. They lost their balance. Jessie, James, and Meowth were thrown out of the opening in the blimp. Desperately, Jessie grabbed on to the torn canvas. A large piece of canvas ripped

off the blimp and ballooned over Team
Rocket like a parachute.

Jigglypuff lost its balance, too. The
Pokémon stumbled off the beam, then
gently landed on top of Team Rocket's
parachute and continued its song.

The blimp passed through the storm
cloud. A clear blue sky peeked through the
hole in the canvas.

"It looks like our problems are over," Ash

said, relieved. "Team Rocket is gone. The ghost turned out to be Jigglypuff. We've got nothing to worry about."

"Don't be so sure," Brock said. "Remember, there's no one piloting this thing!"

"Right!" Ash said. He scrambled down the ladder.

Pikachu, Brock and Misty followed Ash through the blimp. Finally, Ash saw a door marked "Control Room" and burst in.

A control panel with all kinds of buttons and levers sat in the centre of the room. A large window showed the view from the front of the blimp. The blimp was moving swiftly through the air. Through the window, Ash saw a sandy beach dotted with palm trees.

"That must be Valencia Island," Ash said. "But how do we get there?"

"I don't think we have to worry about that," Brock said. "Hang on!"

Ash grabbed on to the control panel as the blimp took a nosedive.

Through the window, Ash saw the island get closer and closer with each passing second.

"Oh, no!" Ash yelled. "We're going to crash!"

CHAPTER 5

THE GS BALL

Ash closed his eyes and braced for the impact.

The blimp shook violently.

Wham! The airship skidded on to the sandy beach. Ash gripped the control panel tightly. He tried to hang on as the blimp raced along the sand.

Then suddenly, the blimp crashed to a

stop. Ash cautiously opened his eyes and looked out the window. They had collided with a cluster of palm trees.

"Is everybody all right?" Ash asked.

"Fine," Brock said, standing up.

"I'm OK," Misty said. "Togepi, too."

"Pika!" replied Pikachu.

They checked to make sure that their Poké Balls were safe.

"Great," Ash said. "Then let's get out of this wreck."

The friends climbed out of the broken airship and on to the beach. Ash saw that a long trail lined by trees edged the coastline.

"Let's go," Ash said, hoisting his knapsack on his back.

"Where exactly are we going?" Misty asked.

Ash stopped. "Uh, don't you guys know where Professor Ivy's lab is?" he asked.

Misty and Brock shook their heads.

Ash sighed. "I guess we'll have to walk until we find something."

Misty, Brock, and Pikachu followed Ash down the trail. They walked for a while, with nothing but blue ocean and palm trees in sight. Ash was beginning to get discouraged when Pikachu piped up.

"Pika!" said the Pokémon, pointing excitedly.

Ash looked. Through the trees he saw a small building made of bamboo. A carved wooden Poké Ball hung over the door.

"Looks like a Pokémon Center," Ash said.

The friends left the trail and walked into the building. A red-haired woman in a nurse's uniform stood behind a desk.

"Welcome to the Pokémon Center," she said. "I'm Nurse Joy."

"Some things never change," Ash said. So far, there was a Nurse Joy in every Pokémon Center he had visited. They all looked alike.

"Can you tell us how to get to Professor Ivy's laboratory?" Ash asked.

"It's very easy," Nurse Joy replied. "Just go out of the Pokémon Center, make the first left, and it's the big white building at the end of the road."

"Thanks!" Ash said.

They followed Nurse Joy's directions and soon found themselves in front of Professor Ivy's lab. The front door was wide open.

"Is anybody home?" Ash asked. He cautiously stepped

inside.

"It looks empty," Brock remarked, following Ash into the room. "We'd better – ow!"

A wooden trapdoor opened, smacking Brock in the head.

Three teenage girls popped their heads out of the doorway.

The girls looked a lot alike. They all had curly hair tied in ponytails, and they all wore glasses. Each wore a bright tropical

shirt in a different colour.

The girls stepped out of the trapdoor.

"I'm Charity," said the girl in the orange shirt.

"I'm Faith," said the girl in the pink shirt.

"I'm Hope," said the girl in the green shirt. "And who are you?"

"We came here to see Professor Ivy," Brock said, smiling at the girls and rubbing his head in pain.

"Professor Oak from Pallet Town sent us," Ash added.

"Professor Ivy is out in the bay," Charity said.

"Follow us!" the girls said together.

The three girls led Ash, Misty, Brock and Pikachu through the building to a back door. The door opened on to a sandy trail that led to the ocean.

Waves crashed on the shore of the empty beach.

"Where's Professor Ivy?" Ash asked.

A loud roar answered him. A giant blue Pokémon that looked like a sea serpent rose out of the ocean.

"A Gyarados!" Ash cried in shock.

Then Ash noticed something unusual about the Gyarados. A woman rode on its back. She had short brown hair.

The Gyarados gracefully swam to shore. The woman climbed off its back and patted its neck. "Very good, Gyarados," she said.

Ash couldn't believe it. Every Gyarados he had ever met was fierce and wild. He couldn't imagine anyone taming one like that.

"Professor Ivy," Charity said. "Three friends of Professor Oak are here."

Professor Ivy put on a white lab coat and smiled.

"Pleased to meet you," she said, holding out her hand.

Brock blushed.

"Professor Oak sent us to pick up that new Poké Ball you found," Ash said.

"Of course," Professor Ivy said. "I'll take you to it."

Ash and the others followed the professor

to a lab inside the building. A Poké Ball sat on a metal table. It didn't look like the red-and-white Poké Balls Ash was used to. This one was half gold and half silver. And there was some kind of writing carved into it. Ash squinted to read it.

"If you look closely, you can see the letters G and S," Professor Ivy said. "That's why we decided to call it the GS Ball."

"We heard that you can't transport it,"

Brock said, staring at it.

"True," Professor Ivy answered. "Would you like a demonstration?"

"Sure," Ash said. He put the GS Ball on top of a Poké Ball transporter in the lab. Normally, Ash would press a button and the Poké Ball would disappear, transported to another lab. That's how Pokémon Trainers sent the Pokémon they caught to storage. No Trainer could carry more than six Pokémon at a time.

Ash put the GS Ball on the transporter pad. He pressed the button. Beams of light hit the GS Ball, but the light crackled sharply on contact. The GS Ball didn't disappear.

"We've tried to open it," Professor Ivy said. "We tried buzz saws, hammers, crowbars, hacksaws, power drills and lasers."

"Nothing works!" said the three girls.

"Wow," Ash said, staring at the gold-and-silver ball. "This thing really is mysterious."

Professor Ivy handed the GS Ball to Ash.

"You're right, Ash," she said. "And now it's up to you to get it safely to Professor Oak."

CHAPTER 6

VILEPLUME

"I won't fail you," Ash said. "We'll go right now."

"Right now?" Brock asked with disappointment in his voice.

"Don't be silly," Professor Ivy said. "It will be dark soon. Stay the night, and I'll show you some of the work we're doing here."

"We'd love to stay!" Brock said quickly.

"Then it's settled," Professor Ivy said. "Let me show you around while Faith, Hope, and Charity prepare the Pokémon food."

Professor Ivy led Ash and the others outdoors to an area near the beach. Besides palm trees, lots of green, leafy plants and brightly coloured flowers grew everywhere. Most of the plants looked strange to Ash.

"So this is all part of your laboratory?" Brock asked the professor.

"Yes," she replied. "We need this space for all of the Pokémon. We breed and study so many of them."

Ash noticed that Brock looked impressed. His friend's dream was to learn how to become a great Pokémon Breeder, Ash knew. This place must seem like paradise to him.

A few feet away, Misty was sniffing some

big, unusual flowers.

"Just look at these!" Misty said admiringly.

Ash watched as Misty bent down to look at them more closely, then jumped back.

The plant began to walk. Startled, Ash realised that it wasn't a plant at all, but a Pokémon. The Pokémon had a round blue body and walked on two legs. On top of its body was a flower with five round, orange petals. The flowers had strange red markings on them.

"A Vileplume!" Brock exclaimed.

Ash took out Dexter, his Pokédex. This handheld computer stored information about all kinds of Pokémon in it. It also served

as his Trainer ID. A picture of a Vileplume appeared on the screen. But the Vileplume in his Pokédex had red petals with pink dots on them instead of orange petals with red markings.

"That's odd," Ash said. "This Vileplume looks different from the one in my Pokédex."

"Time for dinner!" loud voices cried. Faith, Hope and Charity wheeled in a cart loaded with bowls of Pokémon food. At their arrival, several Pokémon began to emerge from the trees.

Ash recognised them. There was a Paras, a Pokémon that looked like a small crab. There were male and female Nidoran, two tough-looking Pokémon with horns on their heads. There was a Weepinbell, a plant-like Pokémon. And there was a Raticate, a rat-like Pokémon with sharp teeth. But even though he recognised them, there was something a little different about each one.

Instead of yellow dots, the Paras was covered with orange triangles. The female Nidoran was a deeper blue than usual, and the male Nidoran had blue inside its ears instead of green. The Weepinbell was orange instead of its usual yellow. And the Raticate had reddish fur instead of its usual brown fur.

"Hey, Professor, why do these Pokémon look a little bit different?" Ash asked.

"It's because of this island's tropical climate," Professor Ivy explained. "The environment creates differences in the Pokémon that we've raised here."

"You mean you've raised all these Pokémon yourself?" Brock asked.

"That's right," Professor Ivy replied. "I've dedicated myself to them, and I couldn't be happier."

Ash heard a stirring in one of the trees. A Butterfree, a Flying-type Pokémon that looked like a large butterfly, flew down from a branch and landed on the food cart. It sniffed the food, then flew back up to the branch and moaned slightly. Ash thought it looked weak.

"That little Butterfree hasn't eaten a thing in days," Professor Ivy said.

"But we've tried five different combinations of nutrients!" Charity said.

Brock approached the food bowl. He sniffed the food, then grabbed a handful and tasted it. He looked thoughtful.

"I've got it!" Brock said finally.

Brock rummaged through his knapsack.

He pulled out some food containers and
began to mix some ingredients in a bowl.
Then he sprinkled the mixture on top of
the Pokémon food.

The Butterfree immediately perked up. It
flew back down and started to hungrily eat
the food in the bowl.

"That's simply amazing!" Professor Ivy said.

Brock blushed. "I noticed that Butterfree
like sweet things, so if you just add some

mashed-up Berries to their food, they'll eat up every time."

"You know a lot about Pokémon feeding habits," Professor Ivy said. "I bet I could learn a lot from you."

Brock blushed even deeper.

"Will you teach us all about the different flavours Pokémon like?" Charity asked.

"Please, Brock!" Faith pleaded.

"Not now," Hope said. "We have to decide who gets stuck cooking dinner tonight."

Brock's face lit up. "Cooking? I love to cook!"

"Then follow us!" said the professor's three assistants.

Ash and the others followed Faith, Hope and Charity into the building and to a living area.

Ash couldn't believe it. Piles and piles

of dirty dishes filled the kitchen area. In the living room, clothes and empty food wrappers covered the floors and furniture.

Professor Ivy shrugged. "We get so wrapped up in our Pokémon work that we don't have time to clean," she said. "We call this place our little dump."

"Dumps are a lot cleaner!" Ash remarked.

But Brock looked thrilled. He rolled up his sleeves and began to clean the rooms with amazing speed. Professor Ivy and her assistants looked shocked.

"Brock loves this stuff," Ash explained. "He spent the last few years at the Pewter City Gym, taking care of his nine brothers and sisters."

In no time, Brock had the rooms sparkling clean, and a delicious dinner was cooking on the stove. The group hungrily ate the meal, then rolled out their sleeping bags in the living room.

"Good night," Professor Ivy said. "I've got some more research to do, but I'll see you in the morning."

"Professor Ivy is so nice," Misty remarked as she snuggled into her sleeping bag. "She's smart, too."

"Yeah," Ash said, yawning. "This place is great. I'm going to miss it."

Brock didn't say anything. He stared out of the window.

Ash and Misty fell asleep in no time. But Brock couldn't sleep. He got up and walked to the outdoor lab.

Brock found Professor Ivy and her assistants crouched behind a leafy bush. Faith held a video camera.

"Get down, Brock," Professor Ivy

whispered. "We're studying the Vileplume. They're nocturnal Pokémon, and at night they all come out and spray their pollen to prevent other Pokémon from entering their territory."

A group of six Vileplume were walking through the trees.

Suddenly, Faith gasped. "Oh, no!" she cried. "Here comes a Raticate!"

The furry Pokémon was walking right into the Vileplume.

"Raticate, no!" Professor Ivy yelled. She jumped from behind the bush and covered the Raticate with her body. At the same moment, the Vileplume shot a filmy yellow powder

from the flowers on their backs. The pollen covered Professor Ivy. She collapsed to the ground.

"Save ... the ... Raticate," she said weakly.

"She was trying to protect the Raticate," Faith said. "The Vileplume's pollen is poisonous to Pokémon."

Brock lifted Professor Ivy in his arms. "It's poisonous to humans, too," he said. "We've got to get her to the Pokémon Center!"

CHAPTER 7

FAREWELL TO A FRIEND

"Is Professor Ivy going to be all right?"
Ash asked. He sleepily rubbed his eyes.
Brock had just woken them all to tell them
about Professor Ivy's encounter with the
Vileplume. They stood in the lobby of the
Pokémon Center, waiting for news.

"I hope so," Brock said, sounding worried.

"What exactly happened out there?" Misty asked.

"The Vileplume were spraying their pollen to mark their territory," Brock explained. "Professor Ivy tried to save a Raticate from being sprayed, and she got hit herself."

"Wow! She really cares about Pokémon," Ash remarked.

The doors leading to the hospital ward swung open. Nurse Joy came out, carrying the Raticate in her arms. Professor Ivy followed them, flanked by Faith, Hope and Charity.

"Professor Ivy," Brock said, "we were so worried about you."

The professor smiled. "I'm fine," she said. "And so is the Raticate."

The rising sun streamed through the lobby windows. Ash stretched and hoisted his knapsack on his back.

"I'm glad you're not hurt," Ash said. "We'll tell Professor Oak when we give him the GS Ball. Are you guys ready to go?"

Misty picked up Togepi. "Sure," she said.

"Pika!" Pikachu agreed.

Brock hesitated.

"Uh, Ash, Misty," Brock said. "I think I'm going to stay here."

"Yay!" cried Faith, Hope and Charity.

Ash couldn't believe it. "You mean you're not coming with us?"

Brock shook his head. "Ash, you know becoming a great Pokémon Breeder is my dream. I could learn so much here."

"And we could learn a lot from you, too," Professor Ivy added. "We'd be happy if you stayed, Brock."

As they talked, they walked outside the

Pokémon Center. The Butterfree Brock had fed yesterday landed on Brock's shoulder and cooed happily.

Brock smiled. "I think these guys need me a lot more than you guys do right now," he said.

Ash wasn't so sure of that. He had grown to depend on Brock's experience.

"Well, then ..." Ash said slowly. "I guess this is goodbye. We'll miss you."

Brock held out his hand. "Friends to the end, right, Ash?"

Ash shook Brock's hand. "Right!"

"Pika!" Pikachu leaped up and hugged Brock.

The group walked to the main trail.

"Bye, Brock!" Misty said.

Brock waved. "Goodbye, everybody!" he called out. "Just don't forget me!"

"We won't!" Ash and Misty called back.

Ash walked backwards along the trail, watching Brock get smaller and smaller in the distance. Finally he couldn't see his friend at all.

"It's going to be really weird not having Brock around," Misty said sadly.

"I know," Ash agreed. "I wish he was coming back with us."

"Now that you mention it, how are we going to get back?" Misty asked.

Ash reached in his pocket. "No problem,"

he said. "I have our blimp tickets right here!"

"Ash, we can't go back on that blimp," Misty protested.

"I guess you're right," Ash said. "The food was bad, and they didn't show a movie."

Misty's face turned bright red. "Ash Ketchum, you are impossible! I should have stayed at the lab with Brock and – hey!"

Misty slammed into Ash as he stopped short. They looked up. A large blimp sat on the beach at the end of the trail. It didn't look like the first blimp. This one looked shiny and new.

Before Ash could say anything, two men in navy blue uniforms jumped in front of them. They both had moustaches.

"Hello!" said one man. "Welcome aboard!"

"Step right up," said the other. "We're

almost ready for takeoff."

Misty looked at the men suspiciously. "Is this thing safe?" she asked.

"This is the safest blimp ever to sail the seven skies," said the first man. "Now get on board!"

The two men shoved Ash, Misty and Pikachu up the steps and into a small room. In the centre of the room were four comfortable-looking seats.

Ash sat down and sank into the soft cushions. "This is great, Misty," he said. "Lots better than the last blimp. We've got nothing to worry about."

The uniformed men disappeared. In minutes, Ash heard the blimp's engines roar as the aircraft lifted into the sky.

"This time, I'm going to make sure I get everything the contest guys promised," Ash said. He raised his voice. "Hey! Where's our food?"

The two men entered the room.

"Hungry, are you?" said the first man.

"Well, I hope you like candy," said the other. "As in bars!"

Suddenly, a cage lined with iron bars dropped from the ceiling and surrounded Ash, Misty, and Pikachu in their seats.

At the same time, the men ripped off their fake moustaches. They peeled off their blue uniforms to reveal familiar white uniforms underneath.

It was Jessie and James!

"Team Rocket!" Ash cried. He jumped up and shook the bars. The cage was solid.

"Meowth! That's right!" Meowth said, jumping into the room.

"Why can't you clowns just leave us alone?"

Misty asked angrily.

Jessie sneered. "We'll
leave you alone
when – hey, where's
that other twerp who
hangs out with you?"

"You mean Brock?"
Ash asked. "He stayed behind."

James grinned. "Jessie, I think we've
trapped two lovebirds in our little cage," he
teased.

Ash and Misty looked at each other.

"You're crazy!" Misty yelled. "Never in a
million years."

"Crazy is right!" Ash said. He had had all
he could take from Team Rocket. "Pikachu,
use your Thunderbolt!"

Pikachu nodded. Sparks sizzled all over its
red cheeks.

"Ash, no!" Misty protested. "Not in the cage."

"Your little girlfriend is right," Jessie said. "The metal bars will conduct the electricity, causing a huge charge. And if even a spark hits the giant gas tank on this thing, we're doomed."

"She's not my girlfriend," Ash protested. "And don't think you've won. I'll find some other way to get us out of here."

"Too late for that," Meowth said, reaching through the bars. "It's time for me to grab Pikachu."

Pikachu dodged Meowth's paws. Ash racked his brain, trying to think of a plan. There had to be some way to escape.

"If Brock were here, he'd figure out a way to get out of this," Misty said.

Ash faced Misty. "I've thought of lots of plans on my own, you know," he snapped.

"Oh, yeah?" Misty said. "So what's your plan now?"

"Aaaaaaaaaaahhh!" screamed Team Rocket.

Ash spun around. Team Rocket looked terrified. A small pink Pokémon was hopping into the room.

Jigglypuff!

"Oh, no," James said. "I thought we ditched that Jigglypuff when we parachuted to the island."

"It must have sneaked on board when we rebuilt the blimp," Jessie guessed.

Jigglypuff looked happy to have a large audience again. It puffed up its pink cheeks and opened its mouth to sing.

"Nooooo!" Team Rocket cried. Jigglypuff's lullaby filled the room. Jessie, James and Meowth quickly grabbed parachutes off the wall. They struggled to put the parachutes on, yawning all the while.

"The ... escape ... hatch," Jessie said.

Ash's eyelids were growing heavy, but he watched as, one by one, Jessie, James and Meowth parachuted off the blimp. Angry, Jigglypuff stopped singing. It jumped after Team Rocket, once again landing safely on Meowth's open parachute.

Ash slumped in his chair. Misty and Pikachu snored on the floor. Jigglypuff was gone, but it was too late.

Ash fell asleep while the blimp sailed on without a pilot!

CHAPTER 8

BATTLE ON THE BEACH

Hours later, a crash woke Ash from his sleep.

Ash's eyes flew open. The crash knocked over the heavy cage. Ash scrambled over to Misty and Pikachu.

"The blimp must have crash-landed while we were sleeping," Ash said. "Are you guys all right?"

Misty opened her eyes. She was still holding Togepi. "I think so," she said. "Just remind me never to travel by blimp again!"

"Pika!" Pikachu agreed. It jumped into Ash's arms.

"Well, at least this blimp got us somewhere," Ash said.

"It sure did," Misty said. "But where?"

Ash swung open the door to the escape hatch. "There's only one way to find out!"

Ash stepped out into the sunlight. Tall green trees rose up around them.

"It looks like we're in the middle of nowhere!" Misty moaned.

"Maybe," Ash said. "But we can't stay here. There's a trail up ahead. Let's go."

Ash, Misty and Pikachu walked on the trail for hours. Just when they were about to give up hope, the trees parted.

Ash squinted in the bright sunlight. The trail led to a small but bustling city along the beach. The ocean sparkled in the distance. As they got closer, Ash saw that hotels, shops, and restaurants dotted the city. Sailboats and motorboats filled the bay.

As they approached the city gates, two women wearing necklaces of bright tropical flowers approached them.

"Welcome to Tangelo Island," they said. One of the women slipped flower necklaces over the heads of Ash, Misty and Pikachu.

"What is this place?" Ash asked.

"It's a Pokémon Resort," one woman said.

"You and your Pokémon can rest, relax, and enjoy yourselves," added the other.

"Sounds good to me," Ash said.

"Me, too!" Misty said.

Pikachu smiled. "Pika pi!"

The friends walked along the beach, enjoying the sunshine. Then Pikachu's smile faded.

"Pikachu!" Pikachu cried, pointing.

Ash looked. A large Pokémon sat on the beach. Ash recognized it. A Lapras. The combination Water- and Ice-type Pokémon looked like a blue beast with a shell on its back. It had four strong flippers. But this Lapras didn't look strong. It lay weakly on the sand.

Three teenage boys surrounded the Lapras. One had spiky green hair. The other wore a bandanna on his head. And the third boy wore a leather jacket. His black hair gleamed with grease.

"Get up and get moving, you lazy lump!" said the boy with the bandanna.

"You better listen," threatened the green-haired boy, "or else!"

Ash cringed as the boy poked the Lapras with a stick. Then Ash got angry.

"Leave that Lapras alone!" Ash yelled, running across the beach.

Misty followed right behind him. "I bet it never did anything to hurt you!" she cried.

The green-haired kid stopped poking the Lapras and faced Ash. "We don't need little

brats like you telling us how to handle our Pokémon."

"Yeah," said the boy in the leather jacket. "We're getting ready for a big battle with the Orange Crew, so get lost!"

Ash and Misty didn't back down.

"I can't believe you guys are Pokémon Trainers," Misty said in disbelief.

"That's none of your business," said the boy in the leather jacket. He reached into his pocket and took out a Poké Ball.

"Go!" yelled the boy, throwing the ball.

The ball opened, and a Spearow flew out. The Normal- and Flying-type Pokémon had a sharp beak and powerful wings.

"Beedrill, let's get buzzy!" said the boy in the bandanna. He threw a Poké Ball, and the Bug- and Poison-type Pokémon whizzed through the air.

"Let's knock 'em out,"
said the green-haired
boy. "Hitmonchan, go!"
He threw a Poké Ball,
and a Fighting-type
Pokémon wearing red
boxing gloves appeared
in a blaze of light.

They were three tough Pokémon, but Ash
stayed calm.

"They don't scare us, do they, Pikachu?"
Ash asked.

Pikachu shook its head.

Pikachu climbed on top of Ash's head. Ash
knew Pikachu would jump off, slam into
the three Pokémon, then hit them with an
electrifying Thunderbolt attack.

The Spearow, Beedrill and Hitmonchan
attacked all at once. They came at Pikachu

with full speed.

Pikachu crouched, then started to leap off Ash's head.

"Hold it!" a voice cried.

The Pokémon stopped abruptly. Ash and the others turned at the sound.

The voice belonged to a boy about Brock's age. He wore a green shirt, red shorts and a red headband in his messy black hair.

The boy was sketching something in a drawing pad.

"This should only take a second," he said, sketching furiously. "Hmmm. This is interesting. The feathers on the Spearow indicate it's not getting enough vitamins. And the colouring on this Beedrill is pretty poor. And it's obvious that this Hitmonchan isn't getting enough exercise."

The three Trainers looked confused.

"These Pokémon are pitifully underdeveloped," continued the boy. He turned to Pikachu. "But this one is perfect! You can tell because its coat is so shiny."

"What do you mean, our Pokémon are underdeveloped?" the green-haired boy asked. Now he and his friends looked angry.

But the boy with the sketchbook ignored him. "Turn a little that way, Pikachu. Great!" He continued to draw.

"We can't let these creeps ignore us," said the boy with the bandanna.

"Let's go, guys!" said his friend in the leather jacket. He pointed to Spearow, Beedrill and Hitmonchan.

The boy with the sketchbook had his back turned to them. The Spearow, Beedrill and Hitmonchan lunged for him. But Ash saw.

"Pikachu, do something!" Ash cried.

Pikachu responded quickly. White bolts of electricity shot from its body. The sizzling blasts shocked the three attacking Pokémon and their Trainers. They collapsed in the sand, dazed.

Pikachu faced them, ready for another Electric attack.

But they had had enough. They recalled their Pokémon and ran down the beach.

"Way to go, Pikachu!" Ash cried. He turned to the boy with the sketchbook. "What did you think of that?"

But the boy wasn't paying any attention. He was crouched over Lapras. In the heat of battle, Ash had forgotten all about the Water- and Ice-type Pokémon.

"We've got to get help," said the boy. "I think Lapras may be really hurt!"

CHAPTER 9

THE LOST LAPRAS

"Take this," said the boy, handing Ash a vial of liquid. "It's for Lapras. I'll get Nurse Joy."

Before Ash could respond, the boy ran down the beach.

Ash turned to Misty. "What should I do?"

"I guess you should give Lapras the medicine," Misty said. "It looks pretty hurt."

Ash opened the vial and held it to the Pokémon's mouth. "Drink this, Lapras," Ash said gently. "It'll make you feel better."

But Lapras used its head to knock away the vial. The medicine flew through the air. Pikachu jumped up and caught it.

"I wonder why it won't take the medicine from me?" Ash said.

Just then, a truck drove down the beach. Ash and Misty helped Nurse Joy and the boy put the Lapras on the platform in the back of the truck. The Lapras was too weak to resist. Then the truck drove away.

"I want to make sure Lapras is all right," Ash said. "Let's go to the Pokémon Center."

By the time Ash, Misty and Pikachu arrived at the centre, Lapras was sleeping in an outdoor pool. Nurse Joy watched Lapras carefully. The boy from the beach was sketching the Pokémon.

"How is Lapras doing?" Ash asked.

"There weren't any serious injuries," Nurse Joy replied. "Lapras will be fine after a rest."

"That's good news!" Misty said, relieved.

"There is a problem," Nurse Joy said. "That Lapras is afraid to have any kind of contact with people at all."

"No wonder," Misty remarked, "after the way those guys were treating it."

"That's too bad," said the boy with the sketchbook. "Especially because it's just an infant."

"That's a baby Lapras?" Ash asked. "But it looks so big!"

"Lapras are large Pokémon," the boy said. "Big schools of Lapras pass by the island this time every year. This one must have become separated from its group."

Ash was impressed. "Sounds like you know a lot about Pokémon," he said.

"Well, you learn a lot being a Pokémon Watcher," replied the boy. He held out his hand. "My name's Tracey."

"I'm Ash, and I'm going to become a Pokémon Master," Ash said, shaking Tracey's hand. "So what does a Pokémon Watcher do?"

"We travel the world, looking for Pokémon so we can study their characteristics and abilities," Tracey said. "We even search for new, undiscovered Pokémon."

"Cool," Ash said.

"I think so, too," Misty said. "My name's Misty. And this is Togepi."

"Nice to meet you," Tracey said.

"Now that we all know one another, what do you say we try getting that Lapras back in the ocean where it belongs?" Ash suggested.

"Count me in!" Tracey said.

"Let's ask Nurse Joy for her advice," Misty said.

They all went inside the Pokémon Center, where Nurse Joy was stationed at the front desk. Two little boys and a girl crowded around Nurse Joy.

"My Starmie needs a check-up," said the little girl. "I want to challenge the Orange Crew."

"Those guys on the beach talked about the Orange Crew, too," Ash told Tracey. "What's that about?"

"The Orange Crew is the name for the Gym Leaders here in the Orange Islands," Tracey explained. "Trainers can't compete in the Orange League until they battle everybody in the Orange Crew."

"I didn't know there was a Pokémon League on the Orange Islands," Ash said. "I've already competed in the league back home. The Orange League would be the perfect challenge for me!"

Misty rolled her eyes. "Ash, we can't hang around here. We have to get that GS Ball back to Professor Oak."

Ash had almost forgotten. The GS Ball was the whole reason for their trip.

"Did you say Professor Oak?" Tracey asked.

He sounded impressed.

Ash didn't notice. He rushed to the videophone in the lobby.

"Hi, Professor Oak," Ash said as his friend's face appeared on the screen.

"Hi, Ash. Hi, Misty," Professor Oak said. "I'm glad you're both OK."

"Yes, we're OK now," Ash said. "We're on Tangelo Island."

"My goodness," the professor said. "That's so far away."

Ash plunged on. "I was wondering, before we bring back the GS Ball, can I compete in the Orange League?" he asked quickly.

The professor looked thoughtful. "Hmm. I'm eager to look at the GS Ball, but competing in the Orange League would be good training for you," he said. "So I suppose it's all right."

Ash cheered. "Thanks, Professor!"

Professor Oak chuckled. "Besides, I know I couldn't stop you if I wanted to!"

The screen went blank.

"I can't believe you know Professor Oak," Tracey said. "He's one of the greatest Pokémon experts in the entire world."

"Well, I'm a pretty important Pokémon Trainer where I come from," Ash said.

Misty coughed.

"I'm lucky to meet a friend of Professor Oak," Tracey said. "Looks like you've got yourself a new buddy!"

Ash, Misty and Pikachu

looked at one another. They weren't expecting this.

"You can't just invite yourself along," Ash protested.

Nurse Joy interrupted them. "The Lapras is awake!" she said.

"Great," Ash said. "Now we can try to get it home."

Tracey got inside the truck and drove it over to the pool to pick up Lapras. Ash, Misty and Pikachu sat in the back.

"Come on, Lapras," Ash said in a gentle voice. "This truck will take you back to the ocean."

"And to your friends," Misty said.

Lapras didn't budge.

"Please, Lapras," Ash pleaded. "We won't hurt you."

But Lapras turned its back on them.

Ash took off his jacket. "I've got to show Lapras it can trust me," Ash said. He jumped into the pool.

Lapras dived under the water. Ash followed it. He tried to get close, but Lapras kept swimming away.

Ash came up for air. "Oh, Lapras," Ash moaned. "Can't you see we're only trying to help you?"

Boom!

Ash jumped at the sound. A round object whizzed through the air. The object smacked into the water, then exploded in pillows of thick grey smoke.

"What's happening?" Tracey cried. Another explosion rocked the pool.

"We're being attacked!" Ash yelled.

CHAPTER 10

SAVE LAPRAS

Jessie, James and Meowth stepped through the cloud of smoke.

"Sorry to interrupt your pool party," Jessie said.

"But we've got a Pokémon to catch!" James finished.

Team Rocket jumped on Lapras's back.

They quickly tied ropes around its neck.

"Meowth! Wait till the boss gets a load of this little baby," Meowth said.

Tracey looked shocked. "Wow, a Meowth that talks human language," he said. "I can't believe it." He took a tape recorder out of his backpack.

Tracey shoved a microphone in front of Meowth's face. "Would you mind if I interviewed you?"

"Well, I'd have to ask my agent," Meowth said.

Jessie knocked the mike out of Tracey's hands. "Can't you see we're busy? We've got a Pokémon to steal!"

Ash jumped out of the pool. "You're not stealing anything!"

James threw a Poké Ball into the air.

"Just try to stop us," he said to Ash.

"Weezing, Smog attack!"

A light flashed, and Weezing appeared. At James's command, thick clouds of black smog poured from its body.

The smog made Ash cough and choke. When it cleared, Ash saw the truck speeding away – with Team Rocket and Lapras on board.

"We'll never catch up to them," Ash said.

Tracey took out a Poké Ball. "No problem. My Venonat can help."

A Pokémon materialised from the ball. The round, furry Pokémon looked like a bug. It had two large red eyes.

"Venonat, use your Radar Eye to track that truck!" Tracey commanded.

Ash watched in amazement as Venonat's eyes glowed with red light. The eyes moved up and down, back and forth. Then they locked in position.

"Venonat's got it!" Tracey said. "Let's go."

Ash grabbed Pikachu. He, Misty and Tracey grabbed three bikes propped up against the Pokémon Center. Tracey put Venonat on his handlebars and led the way.

They pedalled as fast as they could. Soon, the truck was in sight. Ash could see Lapras tied up in the back of the truck. It whined and tried to break free.

"Poor Lapras!" Ash said. "We've got to help it."

Ash pedalled faster, breaking away from Misty and Tracey. Soon he and Pikachu were almost in front of the truck.

"Hang on, Pikachu!" Ash said.

Ash jumped off his bicycle. He and Pikachu smacked on to the bonnet of the truck. Team Rocket screamed in surprise.

Ash stuck his head in the window. "Stop this truck!" he yelled.

"You're not going to stop us, you little twerp!" Jessie said.

Ash reached in and tried to grab the steering wheel from Jessie. The truck tore down the road at high speed. Ash didn't know if he could hang on.

"Pikachu!"

Pikachu jumped into the cab through the passenger window. Electric sparks shot from its body. Then Pikachu let loose with a powerful electric blast.

Jessie, James and Meowth screamed and passed out. Jessie slumped down over the steering wheel.

"Good work, Pikachu," Ash said. "But this truck's out of control. Let's go save Lapras."

Ash and Pikachu jumped into the back of the truck. Ash saw that two big bolts connected the platform to the cab. He pulled the bolts with all his might.

The back of the truck disconnected just in time. The cab of the truck plunged forward, toppling over the edge of a high cliff.

"Looks like Team Rocket's falling over again!" Ash heard Jessie, James, and Meowth cry as the cab fell toward the ocean.

Ash was relieved – but just for a second. The back of the truck began to roll backward. Soon it picked up speed.

Ash turned his head. They were headed straight for the other edge of the cliff!

Frantically, Ash looked for a way to stop

the speeding platform. It was no use. Ash quickly untied Lapras. He grabbed Pikachu and climbed on Lapras's back.

"We're going to be OK," Ash said. "We've just got to stick together."

Ash's stomach lurched as the platform reached the edge of the cliff, then flew over the side.

Seconds later, Misty and Tracey arrived at the cliff's edge, out of breath. They looked down.

They saw nothing but blue ocean.

"Ash!" Misty called. "Pikachu!"

"Don't worry," Tracey said. "We'll find them."

With Venonat leading the way, Misty and Tracey climbed down to the beach. They walked up and down the coastline.

"You're positive they're around here,

Venonat?" Tracey asked.

The Pokémon nodded.

Then a figure appeared on the horizon. It swam toward the shore.

Misty and Tracey looked.

It was Lapras! Ash and Pikachu were riding on its back.

The Lapras swam to shore. Ash and Pikachu climbed down. "You made it!" Misty hugged Ash.

"Lapras, too," Tracey said. "Way to go!"

Ash patted Lapras's head. "You put up quite a fight, Lapras," he said, smiling. "But I caught you anyway."

"Did he say caught?" Tracey asked Misty.

Misty shrugged. "He likes to dream."

Ash and his friends decided to rest after their adventure. They relaxed on the beach. Pikachu and Togepi took turns sliding down

Lapras's long neck.

Nurse Joy found them there.

"Thank you for saving Lapras," she said. "It looks like it has decided to join you on your journey."

"That's right," Ash said. "We're going to travel around the Orange Islands together."

"I'll be with them, too!" Tracey added.

Ash sighed. "I guess you can come. It might be useful to have a Pokémon Watcher on board."

"My Pokémon are useful, too," Tracey said. "You've met Venonat. Now meet Marill."

Tracey opened a Poké Ball. A Pokémon that looked like a fat blue mouse appeared. It had big round ears on top of its head.

"How cute," Misty said.

"I've never heard of a Marill before," Ash said. He took out Dexter.

"Marill, the Water- and Fairy-type Aqua Mouse Pokémon," said Dexter the Pokédex. "Its large ears can hear distant sounds, and the rubbery tip of its tail can expand and contract, assisting Marill in water."

Tracey beamed with pride. "Marill has always been a big help to me," he said. "It can distinguish the cries of Pokémon at great distances."

Pikachu and Togepi hopped up and smiled at the new Pokémon.

Ash grinned, too.

"I guess we're ready to go, then," Ash said. "It looks like the Orange Islands will be our biggest adventure yet!"

The End

"I wonder what kinds of Pokémon we'll see here in the Orange Islands," Ash Ketchum said. "I bet we find rare Pokémon that no one has ever seen before."

"We've already met some amazing new Pokémon," his friend Misty replied. "I can't believe we're riding on a Lapras!"

Ash smiled and patted the head of the large, blue Water-type Pokémon they were sitting on. He had befriended the Lapras, and the friendly creature had agreed to travel with Ash and his friends. Besides Ash and Misty, Lapras carried three other passengers: Pikachu, Ash's Electric-type Pokémon; Togepi, a baby Pokémon that Misty brought with her everywhere; and Tracey, a Pokémon Watcher.

Ash had been to many new places and had had many adventures since he began catching and training Pokémon on his tenth birthday. But travelling around the Orange Islands was turning out to be the most interesting – and the most exciting – yet.

It started as a favour to his friend, Professor Oak. Ash travelled to the islands to see Professor Ivy. She gave him a GS Ball, a mysterious Poké Ball Professor Oak wanted to study. Then his good friend Brock had decided to stay with Professor Ivy and help her with her work. Ash was sad to leave Brock, but he soon met Tracey and found Lapras. He didn't know what would happen next.

"I certainly hope we find some new Pokémon on our journey," Tracey said. "It's always exciting to study something new."

As he spoke, Tracey sketched in a pad. The tall boy was a few years older than Ash. He always wore shorts and athletic shoes so he could easily keep up with any new Pokémon he found. And he always sketched what he saw. Ash peered over his shoulder. Tracey was sketching the Lapras. The drawing was a good likeness of the Pokémon, with its long neck, four strong flippers and a hard shell on its back.

"You can study all you want," Ash said. "But I'm going to catch any Pokémon that I find." To become a Pokémon Master, Ash knew he would have to catch and train all kinds of Pokémon.

Misty rolled her eyes. "Ash, don't you ever think of anything besides catching Pokémon?" she complained.

"Sure," Ash replied. "Sometimes I think about training Pokémon, too."

Misty groaned.

"Pika pika!" Pikachu cried suddenly. The yellow Pokémon pointed at something in the water.

"What is it, Pikachu?" Ash asked.

Lapras swam closer to the object.

"It's a bottle," Ash said. "And it looks like there's a message inside!"

Lapras picked up the bottle with its mouth. Its long neck craned around, and Ash took the bottle from it.

"Thanks, Lapras," Ash said. Excited, he quickly opened the bottle and took out a piece of paper. He unrolled it and read the message aloud.

"'If you know anything about a Pokémon called the Crystal Onix, please tell me,'" Ash read. "It's signed 'Marissa from Sunburst Island.'"

"A Crystal Onix?" Misty asked.

"It's an Onix made entirely of clear crystal," Tracey said. "Normally this Rock-type Pokémon is made of hard, grey rock."

Ash knew that. Brock had used his Onix often in battle. But a Crystal Onix?

"Is there really such a thing?" Ash asked.

"I'm not sure," Tracey said thoughtfully. "Several people claim to have seen it. It's probably just some tall tale."

"Well, I'd sure like to see a Crystal Onix," Ash said. "How about you, Pikachu?"

Pikachu nodded.

"Laaaaaaaaa." Lapras let out a low cry.

Ash looked. A small island jutted out of the water up ahead. "That's Sunburst Island," Tracey said.

"Whoever sent that message lives on Sunburst Island," Misty pointed out.

Ash didn't have to think twice. He was looking for an opportunity to find new Pokémon, and one had fallen right into his lap.

"Next stop, Sunburst Island!" Ash cried. "Let's go find that Crystal Onix."

READ
POKÉMON PERIL
TO FIND OUT WHAT HAPPENS NEXT!

POKÉ RAP!

I want to be the very best there ever was
To beat all the rest, yeah, that's my cause
Catch 'em, Catch 'em, Gotta catch 'em all
Pokémon I'll search across the land
Look far and wide
Release from my hand
The power that's inside
Catch 'em, Catch 'em, Gotta catch 'em all, Pokémon!
Gotta catch 'em all, Gotta catch 'em all
Gotta catch 'em all, Gotta catch 'em all
At least one hundred and fifty or more to see
To be a Pokémon Master is my destiny
Catch 'em, Catch 'em, Gotta catch 'em all
Gotta catch 'em all, Pokémon! (repeat three times)

CAN YOU RAP ALL 150?
HERE'S THE NEXT 32 POKÉMON.
CATCH THE NEXT BOOK, POKÉMON PERIL,
FOR MORE OF THE POKÉ RAP.

Electrode, Diglett, Nidoran, Mankey
Venusaur, Rattata, Fearow, Pidgey
Seaking, Jolteon, Dragonite, Gastly
Ponyta, Vaporeon, Poliwrath, Butterfree
Venomoth, Poliwag, Nidorino, Golduck
Ivysaur, Grimer, Victreebel, Moltres
Nidoking, Farfetch'd, Abra, Jigglypuff
Kingler, Rhyhorn, Clefable, Wigglytuff!

Gotta catch 'em all!

WHICH POKÉMON DID YOU
FIND IN THIS ADVENTURE?

☐ VILEPLUME   ☐ TOGEPI   ☐ LAPRAS

Find information on these and all the other Pokémon
in the Official Pokémon Encyclopedia!

ENCYCLOPEDIA

OFFICIAL PRODUCT